THE BEAR WHO LOVED PUCCINI

by Arnold Sundgaard

illustrated by Dominic Catalano

Philomel Books • New York

Ad - di - o, fio-ri-to asi

For my mother who sang to us.
—A. S.

To Sara and Grant, always follow your dream.
—D. C.

Text copyright © 1992 by Arnold Sundgaard
Illustrations copyright © 1992 by Dominic Catalano
All rights reserved. This book, or parts thereof, may not be reproduced
in any form without permission in writing from the publisher.
Philomel Books, a division of The Putnam & Grosset Book Group,
200 Madison Avenue, New York, NY 10016
Published simultaneously in Canada. Printed in Hong Kong.
Book design by Gunta Alexander. The text is set in Jamille.
Library of Congress Cataloging-in-Publication Data
Sundgaard, Arnold.   The bear who loved Puccini / Arnold Sundgaard;
illustrated by Dominic Catalano.   p.   cm.   Summary: Barefoot, a
young brown bear in the deep forests of Minnesota, falls in love with the
music of Puccini and goes to the city to pursue a career as an opera
singer.   [1. Bears—Fiction. 2. Opera—Fiction. 3. Singers—Fiction.]
I. Catalano, Dominic, ill.   II. Title.   PZ7.S9575Be   1992   [E]—dc20
91-17400   CIP   AC   ISBN 0-399-22135-2
First Impression

Robert Remsen "Barefoot" Rainfield was the name of a young brown bear who lived with his father and mother in the dark deep forests of northern Minnesota. He had been given his name by Shorty John Sundown, a Chippewa Indian chief who thought it wrong for a bear not to have a name just like the rest of us.

One Saturday afternoon, when Barefoot and his parents were out looking for blackberries along the shores of Seven Beaver Lake, they heard a radio playing on the opposite shore. Someone was singing a beautiful song. Barefoot had never heard anything quite like it before.

"What kind of music is that?" Barefoot asked his father.

"That's what's called an opera," his father said.

"What's an opera, Pop?" Barefoot asked.

"Well, it's like a play with music. People sing a story."

Barefoot sat by the shore and listened to the singing for the rest of the afternoon. He loved it.

The name of the opera was *Madama Butterfly* and the radio announcer said it had been written in Italy almost a hundred years ago by a composer named Giacomo Puccini. (The announcer pronounced this name something like JAH-como PooCHEEny!)

"Poocheeny," Barefoot said to himself. "I like that name."

That evening as Barefoot's mother and father were preparing a light supper of acorns and fiddlehead ferns, they were astonished to hear Barefoot singing one of the songs from *Madama Butterfly.* He seemed to remember every word and note perfectly. His voice was as sweet and pure as the voices they had heard on the radio.

All week long Barefoot's voice soared through the woods as he sang songs from the opera. By the week's end Robert Remsen "Barefoot" Rainfield knew what he would do with his life. When he grew up, he would become an opera singer and dedicate his voice to the music of Puccini.

And so one day when the time came for Barefoot to leave, as all bears must when they are old enough, he went to see Shorty John Sundown, the Indian chief who had given him his name.

"What do you want to do with your life?" the Indian chief asked him.

"More than anything in the world I want to be an opera singer," Barefoot told him. "I love the music of Puccini."

"Puccini? Who's he?" Shorty John asked. "Never heard of him."

Then Barefoot told him the story of the Japanese girl called Madama Butterfly and how she gave her love to Lieutenant Pinkerton of the U.S. Navy. But he went away and married someone else instead, and she died for love. Barefoot even sang a few notes to make the old chief understand.

Shorty John listened in silence. He agreed it was a glorious story, and Barefoot had sung it beautifully. Then, wiping a tear from his eye, he said, "Well, if that's what you want to do more than anything in the world, then do it!"

And so Robert Remsen "Barefoot" Rainfield continued to sing with more determination than ever. Then one fine day in September he said good-bye to his father and mother and set out to seek his fortune as an opera singer in the world of music. His first stop would be St. Paul, capital of Minnesota, far from the forest where he was born.

"Write to us," his mother said, holding back her tears.

"Don't worry," his father said. "He knows how to take care of himself."

But both of them were worried. Barefoot was the first brown bear they had ever heard of who wanted, more than anything in the world, to dedicate his life to the music of Giacomo Puccini.

What will become of him? they wondered. How would it all end?

Soon the forest was far behind him. The bus to St. Paul was filled with strangers. As they sped through the unfamiliar countryside, Barefoot began to feel lonely and a little frightened. What will the city be like? he wondered. He had heard stories of dangers in the streets, and for a moment thought of turning back.

Then he remembered what Shorty John had said to him. "Well, if that's what you want to do more than anything in the world, then do it!"

Finding a place to live in a big city is always a problem for anyone, and for a brown bear it is most difficult of all. But Barefoot solved the problem very simply. He built himself a tepee on the banks of the Mississippi River, just the way Shorty John Sundown had taught him.

But early the next morning he was awakened by the sound of a very loud voice. "Open up in the name of the law," someone was shouting.

"What is it?" Barefoot asked innocently.

"Word's come down from City Hall someone's built a tepee here without a permit," the policeman said.

"That doesn't apply to bears," Barefoot said without flinching. "We're an endangered species."

Harry, the policeman, was stopped in his tracks by that one. He took out his little Green Book and studied it carefully. He couldn't find a thing in it that applied to bears.

"What about employment?" he asked finally. "There's a question here about occupation."

"Put down 'opera singer,'" Barefoot said calmly.

"Opera singer!" Harry shouted. "Do you call that an occupation?"

"I do," said Barefoot without blinking an eye.

Harry slowly backed off as Barefoot stared him down. Then he slammed his Green Book shut and walked away.

The next morning Barefoot went for breakfast at a nearby diner called St. Pete's Elite Cafe. He had a delicious breakfast of buckwheat pancakes with maple syrup. The waitress, called Mimi, was very friendly.

"What brings a bear like you to the big city?" she asked him as she poured some extra syrup on his plate.

Barefoot felt a little shy but he decided to confide in her. "I'm here to start my career," he said. "Do you think I could get work here in St. Pete's Elite Cafe?"

"We've already got a dishwasher," she told him.

"I wasn't thinking of dishwasher," Barefoot said. "I was thinking maybe I could sing."

"Sing what?" Mimi asked him.

"Well, Puccini's my specialty," he said. "I think you'd like Puccini."

Mimi hesitated and then said, "I'll have to ask Ernie. He's the boss." And Mimi left the room.

Soon Ernie, the owner, came in from the kitchen. But before he could say a word, Barefoot burst boldly into song: Lieutenant Pinkerton's first solo on love and fancy.

Barefoot's voice rose pure and clear like that of a skylark in flight. He filled St. Pete's Elite Cafe with a song of such sweetness as to break one's heart.

Ernie could hardly believe his ears. Mimi listened in startled surprise. Even Charley, the dishwasher, left his stack of dishes to listen in awe. When Barefoot finished they all burst into wild applause.

In the discussion that followed, Ernie asked Barefoot what an opera singer would charge to perform at St. Pete's Elite Cafe.

"You can pay me in pancakes," Barefoot told him. "Your buckwheat pancakes are almost as good as my mom's."

They shook hands on that, or rather paws and hands, and it was agreed Barefoot could start performances the following Saturday night.

Ernie made a sign to stand in front.

Mimi helped him with his costume. She put medals and gold braid on one of Ernie's white chef's uniforms to make him look like Lieutenant Pinkerton of the U.S. Navy. Charley helped with the lights. He used the restaurant tomato cans to serve as spotlights. Even Harry, the policeman, offered his services. He said he'd control the crowds at the door.

By the time Barefoot made his entrance there was not an empty chair, stool, or table in the entire room.

And when Barefoot took his final bow, the cheering could be heard all the way to the other shore of the Mississippi.

Word soon spread through the city of the singing bear at St. Pete's Elite. People stood in line for Barefoot's pawprint on their menus. Newspaper headlines featured his name. He was interviewed on television.

As weeks flew by, Barefoot's fame spread across the country, then all the way to Europe. One day, the famous maestro Fabio della Rocca of La Scala opera house in Italy appeared at Ernie's cafe with a contract in hand.

"Come to La Scala," he implored. "We will fly you there on our chartered plane."

"But I have a contract with Ernie," Barefoot said. "He's signed me up for pancakes for a year."

"We'll double the pancakes, triple the maple syrup. We'll make new costumes." Then he added, "La Scala is where Puccini first put *Madama Butterfly* on the stage. It would be a great honor to his memory if you'd come."

"Well, I do love Puccini," Barefoot confessed. "But I'd hate to leave my friends here. They've been very good to me."

"We will fly your friends to Italy for opening night," Fabio della Rocca assured him.

"What about my mother and father?" Barefoot asked.

"Of course. Mama and Papa, too. Bring everyone. Bring them all."

And so it was decided that Robert Remsen "Barefoot" Rainfield, a young brown bear from the deep forests of Minnesota, would sing the music of Puccini at La Scala, the most famous opera house in the world!

High over the Atlantic, the chartered plane sped through the clouds. None of Fabio della Rocca's guests aboard had ever seen the ocean before. From above, it looked wider than the Mississippi and bigger than Seven Beaver Lake.

Barefoot thought it a wonderful thing that he could take his friends on so beautiful a flight. But it would be even more wonderful for him to be singing in a real opera house at last.

He practiced his singing. "Mi-mi-mi-mi-mi," he sang softly to himself.

Mimi, seated next to him, thought he was saying her name and smiled happily.

At the airport in Milan, Italy, Barefoot was greeted by a crowd of frantic paparazzi who snapped many pictures of him. He told the newspaper and television reporters how happy he was to be in the country where so great a man as Giacomo Puccini had been born.

"I love Puccini," Barefoot told them, "and at La Scala I will try to honor his name."

La Scala was filled to overflowing for Barefoot's opening night. His friends and family sat proudly in the box seats Fabio della Rocca had reserved for them. Mimi wore her best dinner uniform with a white lace collar. Ernie wore his chef's hat. Charley wore his dishwasher's apron, freshly starched. Shorty John wore his fine Chippewa Indian feathers. Barefoot's father and mother wore the only coats they'd ever had—and they looked handsome and lovely in them.

Never had a La Scala audience heard the role of Lieutenant Pinkerton sung with such soaring strength and beauty.

When the final curtain fell, and Barefoot took his solo bow, the La Scala audience rose as one to cheer him. "Bravo! Bravo!" they all shouted. Even Madama Butterfly threw kisses from the wings.

At the final round of applause, Barefoot looked out at the sea of faces before him. Dazed with happiness, he wondered for a moment how he—a brown bear from the deep dark forest of Minnesota—had come to sing Puccini on this wonderful stage. And then he remembered what Shorty John had said that day when he told him that more than anything in the world he wanted to be an opera singer.

What Shorty John had said was simply this:

"Well, if that's what you want to do more than anything in the world, then do it!"

And that's exactly what Robert Remsen "Barefoot" Rainfield had done.